LAB ANALYSIS

LAB ANALYSIS

ODYSSEYS

VALERIE BODDEN

CREATIVE EDUCATION · CREATIVE PAPERBACKS

Published by Creative Education and Creative Paperbacks
P.O. Box 227, Mankato, Minnesota 56002
Creative Education and Creative Paperbacks
are imprints of The Creative Company
www.thecreativecompany.us

Design by Blue Design (www.bluedes.com)
Production by Joe Kahnke
Art direction by Rita Marshall
Printed in China

Photographs by Alamy (The Advertising Archives, AF archive,
Contraband Collection, Science Photo Library, GAUTIER
Stephane, Jochen Tack, ZUMA Press, Inc.), iStockphoto
(Alan Crawford, HAYKIRDI, Nicolas Loran), Newscom (BSIP,
REX, FRANCK ROBICHON/EPA), Science Source (Patrick
Landmann, Richard T. Nowitz), Shutterstock (Szasz-Fabian Ilka
Erika, John Hanley, isak55, jurasy, Pressmaster)

Library of Congress Cataloging-in-Publication Data
Names: Bodden, Valerie, author.
Title: Lab analysis / Valerie Bodden.
Series: Odysseys in crime scene science.
Includes bibliographical references and index.
Summary: An in-depth look at how forensic scientists use
chemistry and scientific equipment to examine substances
to solve crimes, employing real-life examples such as civilian
aircraft bombing cases.
Identifiers: LCCN 2016031804 / ISBN 978-1-60818-682-2
(hardcover) / ISBN 978-1-62832-471-6 (pbk) / ISBN 978-1-
56660-718-6 (eBook)

Subjects: LCSH: Chemistry, Forensic—Juvenile literature.
Classification: LCC HV8073.B5925 2017 / DDC 363.25/6—dc23

CCSS: RI 8.1, 2, 3, 4, 5, 8, 10; RI 9-10.1, 2, 3, 4, 5, 8, 10; RI 11-12.1, 2,
3, 4, 5, 10; RST 6-8.1, 2, 5, 6, 10; RST 9-10.1, 2, 5, 6, 10; RST 11-12.1,
2, 5, 6, 10

First Edition HC 9 8 7 6 5 4 3 2 1
First Edition PBK 9 8 7 6 5 4 3 2 1

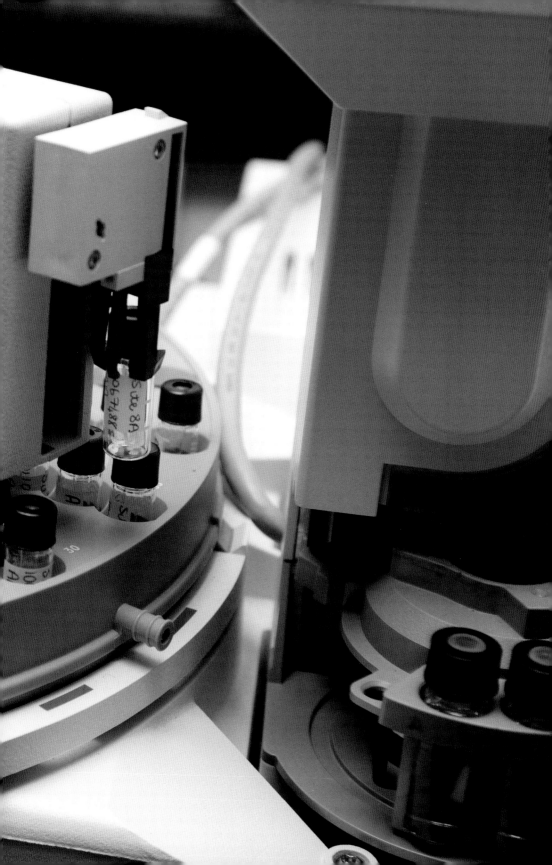

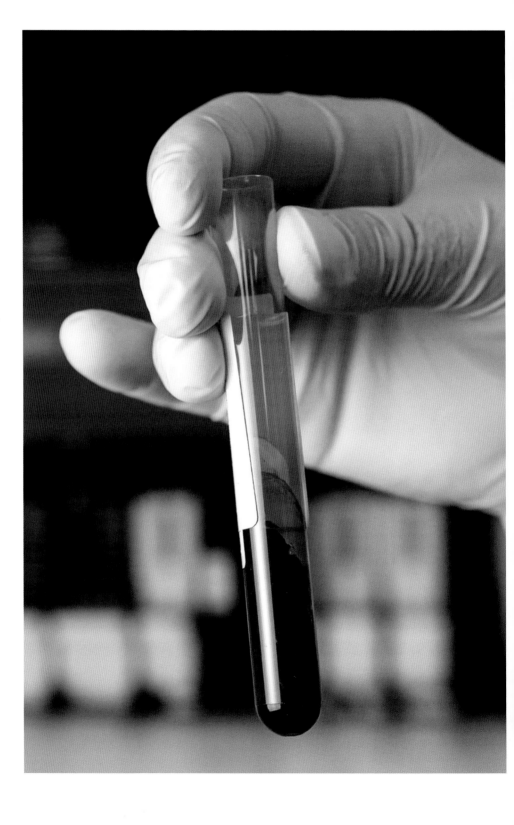

CONTENTS

Introduction

Blue and red lights sweep across the front of a home. They reflect off jagged shards of glass in a broken first-floor window. Inside, books and pictures have been tossed to the floor. Papers hang from ransacked drawers. Two plates—their food still warm—sit on the kitchen table. A small red spot stains the floor under one of the chairs. This looks like a crime scene. But by the time police

OPPOSITE: Many police departments employ a specialized crime scene van to carry the equipment and supplies needed to process a crime scene. The van also transports carefully packaged evidence to crime labs, where forensic scientists examine, test, and analyze the evidence.

arrived, the house was empty. Now investigators must use crime scene science to help solve the mystery of what happened here—and who did it.

Crime scene science is also referred to as forensic science. Forensic science is simply science that is used to solve crimes and provide facts in a legal trial. Solving a crime often involves many forensic scientists, each specializing in a different area. Many of those scientists work in the lab, where they use chemistry to identify unknown substances. Chemistry can be used to detect drugs and poisons. Or it can pick up traces of explosives or chemicals used to fuel fires. Often, identifying these substances is the key to solving a crime.

The Basics

The first step at any crime scene
is to document and collect
evidence. This is the job of crime
scene investigators (CSIs). They
are trained to collect fingerprints,
blood, bullet casings, chemical
residues, and any other evidence
that might help solve the case. But
this evidence means little on its
own. It needs to be analyzed and
interpreted to figure out how it
relates to the crime. That's why

the CSIs package the evidence and send it to a crime lab.

A forensics chemistry lab is home to all kinds of scientific equipment. For some investigations, chemists might rely on tools as simple as a microscope. But other cases require advanced devices, such as **gas chromatographs** and **mass spectrometers**. These devices can identify substances too small to be seen even with the most powerful microscopes. But, "as sophisticated as many of the lab's instruments are, they are only as good as the people who use them," says true-crime author David Fisher. "Machines can only answer those questions that are asked, and the most important aspect of identifying an unknown substance is posing the right question to the right instrument." That's where the forensic chemist comes in.

Chemists study the structure, properties, and reac-

All matter has its own unique chemical structure.... Forensic chemists use such signatures to identify unknown substances.

tions of matter. They look at how **atoms** and **molecules** interact and bond. By looking at the molecular structure of unknown substances, the chemists try to figure out which **compounds** are present. "There are literally 10 million **organic** chemicals," according to Fisher, "and each of those 10 million can be combined with one or more other chemicals to form an infinite number of mixtures. And at some point every case will require that a specimen be analyzed and its composition determined."

All matter has its own unique chemical structure. This is sometimes referred to as its chemical "signature."

Forensic chemists use such signatures to identify unknown substances. In the case of a drug bust, for example, chemists can use cocaine's chemical signature to figure out if a substance is the drug or some other unknown white powder.

Chemistry was the first of the forensic science disciplines to be used in court. In 1751, an English woman named Mary Blandy was accused of poisoning her father with arsenic. A newly developed test detected the poison in his body. Blandy was convicted. From that

It's in the Hair

Anything taken into your body—including drugs or poisons—travels around your system. It even goes to the scalp, where it is deposited in your hair follicles. The part of your hair that grows doesn't have any living cells, so it cannot break down these substances. They are stored in the hair, unchanged. Most people's hair grows at a rate of about half an inch (1.3 cm) a month. Knowing this, toxicologists can make a calendar of every time a drug has been taken since a person's last haircut. Some forensic experts argue that hair analysis is too uncertain. They say that different hair textures, colors, and growth rates can impact how drugs are stored in the hair. Chemicals used for hair coloring and styling may also affect the analysis.

time on, chemistry continued to be used in trials. Over the years, scientists developed more accurate poison detection methods.

The study of poisons and their harmful effect on the body is known as toxicology. Toxicologists test bodily fluids and tissues to find poisons, legal and illegal drugs, gases, or industrial chemicals. Sometimes, toxicology exams are carried out postmortem, or after an individual has died. Postmortem tests can show whether drugs or alcohol played a role in a person's death. The results of

BELOW Medical examiners are responsible for performing autopsies, determining cause of death, and extracting and analyzing toxicological evidence. If the death is considered suspicious, the medical examiner may also be called upon to testify in court.

these tests are used to figure out whether a person was murdered, died as the result of an accident, or committed suicide. Toxicology tests are especially important when an otherwise healthy person dies but shows no signs of trauma. The tests can show whether he ingested poison—and, if so, whether it was accidental or on purpose.

Samples for postmortem toxicology testing are collected by a **medical examiner** during an autopsy. They are then sent to the lab for analysis. Any human tissue can be tested. But blood and urine usually give the best results. Toxicologists also frequently test organs such as the liver, kidney, and brain. They check stomach contents and **bile**, as well as hair and fingernails. Some poisons collect in certain parts of the body. So if a specific chemical is suspected, the toxicologist might test the parts most likely to harbor it. Lead collects in the teeth and ribs, for example. Evidence of inhaled gases is often found in the lungs. Marijuana remains in certain parts of the brain. In cases where a body is burned or severely decomposed, the toxicologist may examine vitreous humor. This is the clear gel that fills the eyeball. It is ideal for testing because it doesn't decompose. Sometimes maggots found on a body are tested as well. Any chemicals present in the body when the insects fed on it will show up in tests.

ot all toxicology exams are carried out after death. Blood and urine samples are often collected from

live suspects or victims. These samples can help determine the role of alcohol or drugs in an accident or a crime. In addition, many workplaces and athletic organizations require routine drug testing.

Testing for impairment—as in the case of drunken driving—needs to be carried out on blood samples. A urine sample cannot provide an accurate time frame for the use of drugs or alcohol. Some drugs can show up in the urine for weeks after use, though. Urine is often used for workplace or athletic drug testing.

Toxicology is not the only use of chemistry in the crime lab. Chemists also test pills, powders, liquids, food, candy, and other substances to check for drugs or poisons. They analyze fire and explosive residue in arson and bombing cases as well.

Most forensic scientists spend all their time in the

lab. But forensic chemists sometimes go into the field to help shut down secret drug labs. These labs often contain hazardous or explosive chemicals. The chemist provides law enforcement with guidance on making the lab safe. He directs the packaging of chemicals and drugs for further testing at the lab.

Wherever they are working, all forensic scientists have to ensure the integrity of the evidence. They have to handle it carefully to avoid **contaminating** it. They must also keep track of the evidence's chain of custody. This is a record of who has the evidence, when they have it, and what they do with it. According to Fisher, "The crime lab is not a place for testing theories or conducting experiments. It's practical, and it's often brutal. It's a place where every test may change someone's life forever."

Disassembling illegal drug labs can be dangerous. In addition to hazardous, unstable chemicals, toxic fumes are often given off through the production process. Police officers and forensic chemists must wear protective suits and gas masks as they work.

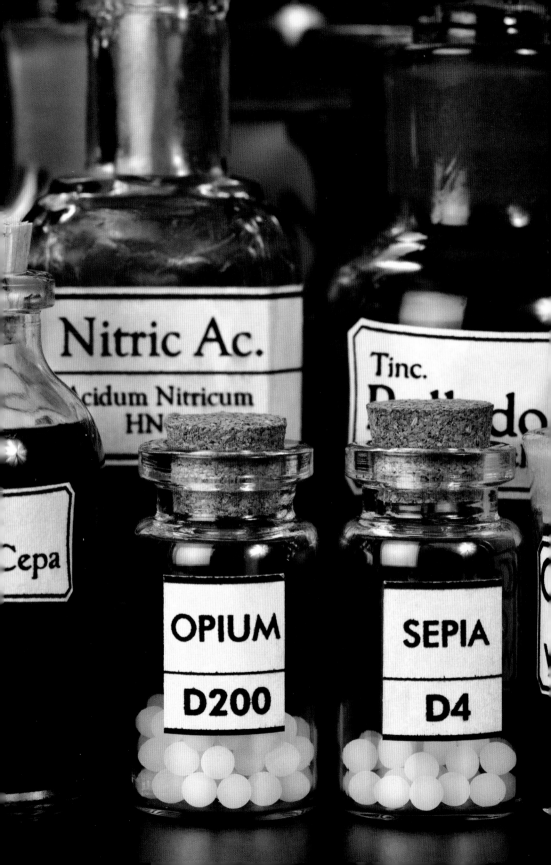

Everything Is a Poison

Forensic toxicologists are mainly concerned with poisons. They define a poison as anything taken into the body that can cause harm or death. Drugs, chemicals, and gases can all be poisons. In fact, anything—even water—can be a poison in a large enough dose.

Most cases of poisoning are accidental, as when a child ingests a household chemical. Drug overdoses

OPPOSITE: Arsenic was once so common that it was known as "inheritance powder." It was often used among royal families to kill off relatives competing for the throne. Because the effects of arsenic poisoning mirrored many common diseases or illnesses, few poisoners were caught.

are also considered accidental poisonings. Other poisonings are self-inflicted, as when an individual uses gas from a vehicle's exhaust pipe to commit suicide. Poisoning was once a common way to kill someone. But the ability of modern tests to detect poisons has led to a steep decline in murder-by-poison. Today, only about 1 in every 100 murders involves poisoning. But it is likely that some murders committed by poison go undetected and unreported.

Most of the work in a forensic chemistry lab goes toward detecting alcohol, prescription medications, and illegal drugs. The substance most commonly tested for is alcohol, especially in cases where someone is suspected of driving under the influence. Because of the high number of alcohol-related cases, most of this testing is automated. In an apparent drug overdose, body tissues may be tested for cocaine, **barbiturates**, and other substances. Because many drugs break down in the body, toxicologists also look for metabolites. These are the compounds each drug breaks down into.

n many cases, chemists are called on to analyze drugs seized during a bust. They may also test for drug residue on objects. In a case in Miami, for example, a young man died of cocaine poisoning after downing a soft drink called Pony Malta. Cocaine residue was found inside the bottle. Investigators soon learned that drug lords had been using the soft drink bottles to smuggle drugs into the United States.

Although drugs and alcohol account for much of the work in the lab, toxicologists do still deal with cases of poisoning. For a killer, the ideal poison is odorless and tasteless. That makes it easier to hide in food or drinks. It is also highly lethal in small doses. Some substances, such as cyanide, cause death instantly. Others, such as arsenic or thallium, are given in small doses over time. After a while, they build up to fatal levels in the victim's body. Many poisons are difficult to detect. A victim's only symptoms might be vomiting or fever. Doctors can easily mistake these as a sign of other illnesses.

Sometimes, a person is thought to have died from natural causes, but suspicions of poisoning are later raised. When Georgia police officer Maurice Glenn Turner died in 1995, for example, doctors said it was

For a killer, the ideal poison is odorless and tasteless. That makes it easier to hide in food or drinks.

from an enlarged heart. His wife Lynn received a large life insurance payment. She soon began seeing another man, Randy Thompson. In 2001, Thompson died, too. The official cause of death was an irregular heartbeat. The two men's families soon became suspicious, however. Both bodies were exhumed. Toxicology exams showed that both men had died of antifreeze poisoning. Lynn was sentenced to life in prison. She died there in 2010 after poisoning herself with a medication overdose.

Whether they are testing for drugs or poisons, toxicologists first put samples through a presumptive, or screening, test. These tests check for the presence of various chemical substances. They can be used in the

OPPOSITE Although screening tests are frequently used to determine the presence of a drug or other substance, the U.S. Food and Drug Administration recommends that further testing be conducted to confirm the presence of the substance.

field or at the lab. For most screening tests, chemical reagents are added to a sample. If the sample changes colors, it means that drugs or poisonous substances might be present. Screening tests for marijuana, for example, turn purple in the presence of the drug. Tests for cocaine turn turquoise. In general, each screening test can detect more than one substance. A screening test for opiates, for example, would produce positive results from morphine, codeine, and heroin. All these drugs belong to the opiate family. Screening tests help forensic scientists narrow down the list of possible drugs in a sample. But sometimes substances other than drugs can cause false positive readings. Nutmeg causes a positive result in marijuana screening tests, for example. In addition, a negative result does not necessarily mean that no drug or poison is present. The sample might contain a substance

You Be the Chemist

You might not be looking for poison, but you can use chemistry to identify your own white powders. First, place 1/4 teaspoon (1.2 ml) each of flour, sugar, baking soda, and cornstarch on separate pieces of black paper. Write down what you notice about each. Next, put a drop of water on each powder. Record any reactions. Then put 1/2 teaspoon (2.5 ml) of each powder into separate clear glasses. Add a few drops of vinegar to each. Note what happens. Finally, place another 1/2 teaspoon (2.5 ml) of each powder in a glass. Add two drops of iodine to each. Record any changes. Now have a friend or family member place one of the powders at a "crime scene." Can you use these tests to identify it?

chemists haven't tested for yet.

If they get a positive result on a screening test, chemists must perform confirmatory tests. These tests are used to identify the specific drug present in a sample. Most often, this is done using gas chromatography and mass spectrometry.

A gas chromatograph separates a substance into its various chemical parts. The sample is first heated until it vaporizes. The vapor is then pushed through a long glass tube with another gas, such as he-

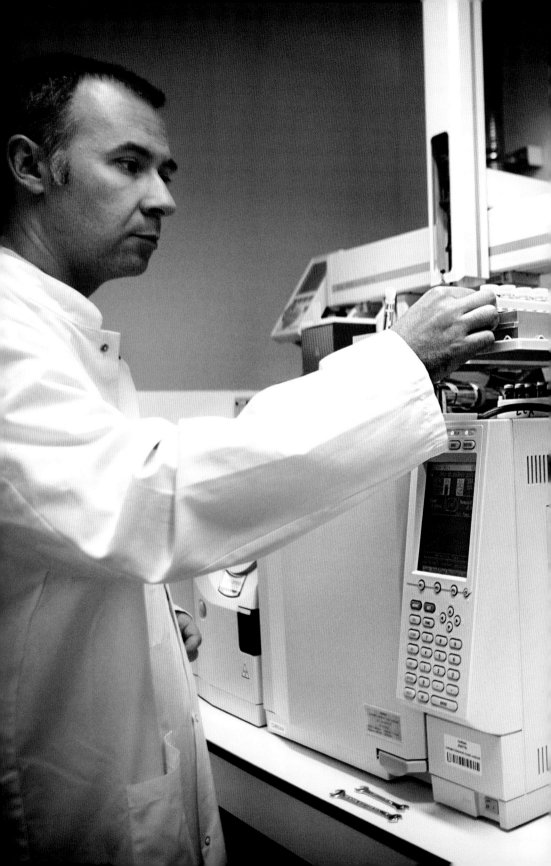

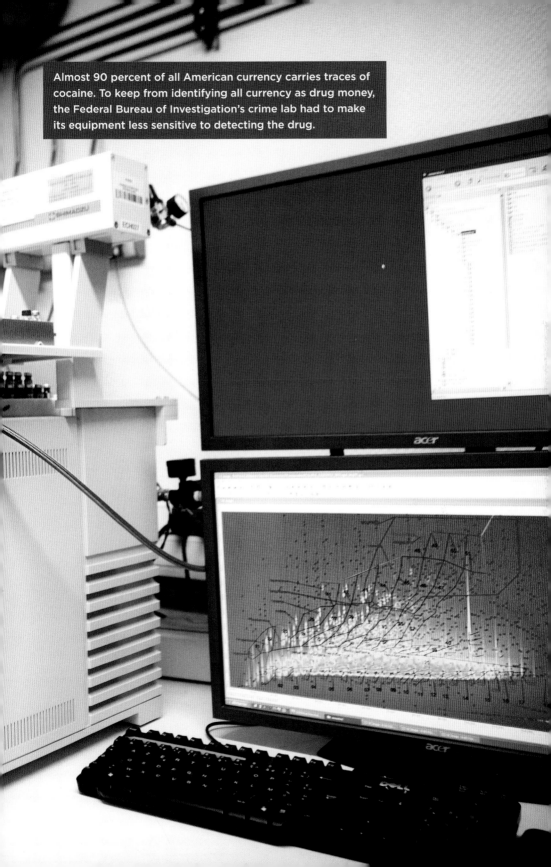

Almost 90 percent of all American currency carries traces of cocaine. To keep from identifying all currency as drug money, the Federal Bureau of Investigation's crime lab had to make its equipment less sensitive to detecting the drug.

lium or nitrogen. As the vapor moves through the tube, its individual components break apart. Each travels at a different speed. The speed at which a component moves can be compared with the known speeds of various substances to identify it.

After the components of a substance are separated, they are often run through a mass spectrometer. This device hits the chemicals with a beam of electrons. This causes each chemical to break apart into ions, or charged particles. The ions are then put through a magnetic or electric field. This makes the ions spread out. Each compound forms a unique pattern, called a mass spectrum. Scientists can then compare the results against the mass spectra of known substances. Confirmatory tests can also be used to determine the amount of each substance in a sample.

Once they have completed testing, toxicologists may be asked to interpret the results. Using their knowledge of how various substances affect the body, they may be able to state the effects of a drug or poison on the individual. Just because tests reveal the use of a drug does not mean the drug caused the person's death. In one case, a 24-year-old man fell from a second-story balcony. Tests showed **designer drugs** and cough medicine in his body. But the toxicologist found that these drugs had not led to his fall.

Where There's Smoke

Chemistry plays a role in arson and explosives investigations. Arson is the crime of purposely setting fire to a home, building, or vehicle. Some people commit arson to hide another crime, such as a murder. They use the fire to destroy the victim's body and other evidence. Other people burn down buildings and then claim that the fire started accidentally in order to collect insurance money. Sometimes,

OPPOSITE: An estimated 22,500 buildings are destroyed by arson every year. Arson investigators sometimes build replicas of burned structures and set fire to them. This can give them an idea of how the original fire acted—and if it was started on purpose.

people burn down a rival's place of business. And some people, known as pyromaniacs, commit arson out of an uncontrollable urge to start fires.

While many crimes are easy to detect—missing money or a dead body, for example—arson may not be apparent. The results of an accidental fire look very similar to those of an intentional fire. Any fire is based on chemistry. The reaction of a fuel and oxygen creates energy in the form of heat and light. In the case of arson, that reaction is often strengthened or hastened by an accelerant, or a liquid fuel that burns easily. Accelerants include gasoline, kerosene, paint thinner, and charcoal lighter fluid. The resulting fire burns off much of the accelerant. But traces of the liquid often remain, even after the fire is out. These traces are what help identify a fire as arson.

The first step in any arson investigation is to collect accelerant residue from the scene. Sometimes a fuel gives off such a strong scent that it can simply be smelled. In some cases, dogs are brought to the scene to sniff out accelerants too faint for humans to detect. Investigators also use portable testing devices to locate accelerants. Some tests change color when exposed to a liquid fuel or its vapors. An ultraviolet lamp can also be shined onto fire debris. Certain substances, such as gasoline residue, will appear to glow when the light hits them. More advanced tests are carried out by catalytic combustion detectors, also known as "sniffers." These devices measure vapors in the air. Some investigators even carry portable gas chromatographs to test residue at the crime scene. Any items thought to contain accelerant residue are packed in airtight metal paint cans or glass jars. This prevents vapors from escaping.

At the lab, chemists can study the tiniest drop of accelerant. But first they may have to extract it from the residue. In some cases, this is done by slowly heating the debris in its container. This vaporizes the accelerant. The vapor is then pulled out using a gastight syringe. Accelerants can also be removed from debris using a strip of activated charcoal. This can absorb traces of the chemical.

Once the accelerant has been separated from the debris, it can be tested using gas chromatography and mass spectrometry. These tests can identify the various chemicals that make up the accelerant. This allows investigators to pinpoint a specific fuel source. The tests are so sensitive that it is sometimes possible for chemists to determine the grade of gasoline. In some cases, they can even pick out the specific gas station where it was purchased. If police have a suspect, they can try to match the accelerant to substances found at the suspect's home, on his clothing, or even in his vehicle's gas tank.

Once a sample of heated vapor has been drawn out of the evidence container, it is run through the gas chromatograph to determine its chemical makeup. From there, investigators can conclude if accelerants were used—and if foul play was involved.

As in an arson investigation, much of the work involved in an explosives case centers around chemistry. In an explosion, a small charge sparks an explosive material. This causes the material to undergo a violent reaction. The reaction produces light, heat, and a pressure wave that pushes gases out in all directions.

Many bombs are homemade and use common and easy-to-get materials as explosives. Mixed with the right ingredients, substances as simple as sugar and weed killer can be used to make a powerful explosion. The 1995 bombing of Oklahoma City's Alfred P. Murrah Federal Building, for example, was caused by fertilizer and fuel oil. The mixture was packed into a truck and set off with an electrical timer. Fertilizer was also used in the 1993 bombing of the World Trade Center in New York City. In addition, it forms the base of many improvised explosive devices (IEDs) used in Iraq, Afghanistan, and other war-torn regions.

Although a bomb sends debris flying in all directions, much of the bomb itself often remains intact. Any undetonated explosive material from the scene gets collected. Investigators also test pieces of the bomb and other debris from near the center of the blast. On-site testing often begins with color-changing reagents. Sniffers and portable gas chromatographs are also used.

Any debris believed to contain explosive residue is

sent to the lab. The residue can be removed from the debris using acetone and other chemical solutions. It is then tested further using gas chromatography and mass spectrometry. These techniques can help the chemist identify the chemicals left behind after an explosive reaction. Based on this information, the chemist tries to figure out the type of explosive from which these materials originated.

The first-ever bombing of a civilian aircraft occurred in 1955. During the investigation, chemists noted the

A Four-Million-Piece Puzzle

On December 21, 1988, Pan Am Flight 103 exploded over Lockerbie, Scotland, killing 270. Investigators collected more than 4 million pieces of wreckage spread across 1,000 square miles (2,590 sq km). Using these pieces, they were able to reconstruct more than 90 percent of the plane. They discovered traces of explosives in the baggage compartment. Debris from this area was tested using gas chromatography and mass spectrometry. This led investigators to conclude that a bomb made of the explosive Semtex had been hidden in a suitcase. Authorities tracked the bomb to Libyan Abdelbaset al-Megrahi. He was convicted of the bombing in 2001. But al-Megrahi maintained his innocence until his death from cancer in 2012. Scottish authorities continue to investigate the incident.

presence of sodium carbonate. They knew the chemical shouldn't be there. But they were unsure how it related to the case. William Magee, a chemist with the Federal Bureau of Investigation (FBI), was involved in the analysis. "Gradually things began to make sense," he later said. "When dynamite explodes, the heat of the blast frees sodium atoms. Sodium atoms like to combine with something—something like carbon dioxide, to form sodium carbonate. Once we'd figured it out, it seemed so obvious. We were looking at the residue of a dynamite explosion; we were holding in our hands the proof that there had been a bomb on that plane. Today, the first thing investigators search for when an airplane goes down or a bomb goes off is explosive residue. But we were working on the first case of sabotage in modern aviation history. We were the people who discovered it would be there."

Chemistry on the Screen

From Shakespeare's *Romeo and Juliet* to the fairy-tale classic *Snow White*, poisoning has played a role in many works of fiction. In crime stories, writers often employ poison as a method of murder. They then set their fictional detectives to work figuring out the identity of the poison—and the poisoner.

Queen of Crime

British writer Agatha Christie once said, "Give me a decent bottle of poison and I'll construct the perfect crime." She used poison as a murder weapon in almost half of her 66 novels. Christie first thought of writing a detective story while working at a pharmacy during World War I. "I began considering what kind of a detective story I could write," she later said. "Since I was surrounded by poison, perhaps it was natural that death by poisoning should be the method I selected." She made notes about the smells and appearances of the substances around her. She wrote that one liquid, called extract of ergot, "smells of bad meat extract." Poisons employed in Christie's novels ranged from arsenic and cyanide to anthrax.

Among the most famous fictional detectives of all is Sherlock Holmes, the creation of Scottish author Sir Arthur Conan Doyle. At a time when real-life forensic science was just beginning, Holmes's scientific methods were groundbreaking. According to his faithful sidekick Dr. Watson, Holmes has a "profound" knowledge of chemistry. He is "well up in belladonna, opium, and poisons generally."

In at least a dozen cases, Holmes must detect the use of poisons. Among the substances Holmes deals with are opium, chloroform, and cyanide. In one case, he even finds a toxin produced by the lion's mane jellyfish. In the very first Holmes novel, *A Study in Scarlet* (1887), Holmes tells Watson how he solved the murder. "Having sniffed the dead man's lips, I detected a slightly sour smell, and I came to the conclusion that he had had poison forced upon him," Holmes says. In the 1893 story "The Naval Treaty," Watson watches as Holmes tests a solution with litmus paper. "'You come at a crisis, Watson,' said he. 'If this paper remains blue, all is well. If it turns red, it means a man's life.' He dipped it into the test tube, and it flushed at once into a dull, dirty crimson. 'Hum! I thought as much!' he cried.... 'A very commonplace little murder.'"

Today, forensic fiction is more popular than ever. With the debut of *CSI: Crime Scene Investigation* in 2000,

TV dramas focusing on the science of solving crimes have risen in popularity. The main character of a crime show today is "likely to be a PhD educated at an Ivy League university," according to author Edward Ricciuti. This character will probably be "more adept at biochemistry ... than in running down and slugging it out with a fleeing criminal." Take Abby Sciuto of *NCIS*, for example. She has a master's degree in criminology and forensic science and a PhD in chemistry. "If Sciuto existed, she might be the most qualified and effective forensic scientist in history," according to journalist Jordan Michael Smith.

As in real life, toxicology often plays a part in television crime investigations. On *CSI*, for example, toxicologists have found arsenic, nicotine, and other substances in victims' remains. They have run tests to tell whether drugs or alcohol played a role in a single-vehicle accident.

And they've even examined insects found on a body. In that case, forensic **entomologist** Gil Grissom explained the science behind the investigation. "Whatever he ingested probably evaporated from the sun, but the maggots are like little refrigerators. They preserve what we digest for longer periods of time." But *CSI*'s investigators know that just because a poisonous substance is found does not necessarily mean that it contributed to a victim's death. In the episode "Friends and Lovers," toxicologists determine that the levels of a toxin found in the victim's blood were too low to have killed him.

Of course, TV doesn't get everything right. For one thing, forensic chemistry on TV is usually more exciting than it is in real life. "Forensic science, it would seem, is a glamorous profession where sharp-minded scientists use state-of-the-art technology," said journalist Bob Doucette.

"At least that's how the television version goes. The reality is those same sharp-minded scientists work long hours, perform tedious work, and labor under less-than-ideal conditions with aging equipment."

Probably the biggest difference between forensic chemistry on TV and the real thing is the time involved. On TV, chemists perform a single test that brings instant results. "Their capabilities on TV are magical," said toxicologist Byron Curtis. In reality, such testing takes an average of four to six weeks. And if the chemical cannot be easily identified, results can take months or even years—especially if new tests have to be created. And what about the on-site analysis that involves an investigator smelling or tasting an unknown substance? Real-life investigators would never do that. "The TV detective who tastes the strange white powder is not only contaminating evidence, he may also end up ... poisoning himself in the process," according to the National Forensic Science Technology Center (NFSTC).

In recent years, some in the legal community have begun to worry that crime shows like *CSI* have given jurors unrealistic expectations of real-life forensic science. They have even come up with a name for this phenomenon: the "*CSI* Effect." Prosecutors claim that the *CSI* Effect negatively impacts cases that don't feature forensic evidence. They say juries are unwilling to convict without

As a result [of the *CSI* Effect], some judges and lawyers have begun to educate juries about the realities of forensic evidence.

such evidence. But defense attorneys argue that jurors see forensic evidence as perfect, which may cause them to ignore other evidence.

As a result, some judges and lawyers have begun to educate juries about the realities of forensic evidence. For example, a judge in one drug trafficking case reminded the jury that they could base their verdict only on evidence presented in court. They could not rely on what they had seen on TV. She pointed out that evidence such as that found on *CSI* was not necessary for a conviction. The jury found the defendant guilty, but he appealed the conviction. He argued that the judge's directions to the jury influenced the verdict. The appeal was denied.

More recently, media attention has shifted to real-life toxicology in some high-profile cases. In 2008, for example, actor Heath Ledger was found dead in his apartment. Toxicologists found numerous prescription painkillers, sleeping pills, and antianxiety medications in his system. They concluded that "the manner of his death is accident, resulting from the abuse of prescription medications." The 2009 death of singer Michael Jackson was determined to have been caused by an overdose of the drug propofol. Because Jackson's doctor gave him the drug, he was imprisoned for involuntary manslaughter. The singer Prince died in 2016 after overdosing on the painkiller fentanyl. Following an autopsy, the medical examiner ruled his death to be accidental. Suffering from hip pain for years, Prince sought help for his increasing dependence on painkillers shortly before his death.

Moving Forward

Once a forensic chemist has finished her analysis, she writes a report. This gets sent to the medical examiner, detectives, prosecutors, and others involved in solving the case. Often, this is the last the chemist hears of the case. But sometimes, forensic chemists are called to court. They might be asked about whether a poison contributed to a person's death. Or they may need to describe how a drug dosage would affect a

OPPOSITE: Although forensic chemists spend the majority of their time in the lab testing and analyzing substances and thoroughly detailing results, they must also be prepared to give expert testimony in a trial.

65

In recent years, the practices of many forensics labs have been called into question.

person of a certain height, weight, and age.

In addition to the communication skills necessary for court appearances, forensic chemists generally need a bachelor's degree in chemistry, forensic science, or a related field. Many forensic chemists also hold advanced degrees. On-the-job training is a requirement for most forensic chemistry jobs as well. So is continuing education and research.

Most forensic chemists are civilians. But some are police officers. The majority of forensic chemists work in federal, state, or local law enforcement labs. Others work in medical examiners' offices. Some forensic chemists also work in hospitals, universities, or private labs.

Wherever they work, forensic chemists have to take precautions when examining bodily fluids or potentially harmful chemicals.

I
n recent years, the practices of many forensics labs have been called into question. In 2009, the National Academy of Sciences (NAS) released a report on the state of forensic science. The report questioned the scientific method behind many disciplines. But forensic chemistry was upheld as a "mature forensic science discipline and one of the areas with a strong scientific underpinning." Still, forensic chemistry is only

as good as the scientists practicing it.

In some cases, these scientists lack the training necessary to perform their jobs well. Most labs require forensic chemists to have a degree in the field. But there is no law setting minimum qualifications for lab workers. "If they started requiring labs to be led by scientists, 60 to 70 percent would have to close down immediately," criminologist Brent Turvey said. This lack of training has led to quality control issues in labs across the country. A crime lab in St. Paul, Minnesota, for example, was temporarily closed after investigators discovered dirty equipment and incorrect testing techniques. "These people didn't know what they were doing," said assistant public defender Lauri Traub. "They had no business running a lab in the first place. And yet they came into court every day and acted as if they did."

Getting It Wrong

In January 1991, Patricia Stallings was convicted of poisoning her four-month-old son with ethylene glycol, or antifreeze. But a second analysis showed that the substance found in the boy's body was not ethylene glycol. It was propionic acid. This chemical was produced by the boy's body as the result of a **genetic** disorder. Toxicologists said it would have been impossible for the boy to have ingested the amount of ethylene glycol the original analysis claimed was in his blood. The baby would have had to swallow 80 gallons (303 l) of antifreeze! "I couldn't believe that somebody would let [these results] go through a criminal trial unchallenged," said Piero Rinaldo, a genetics expert who helped with the case. Stallings was released from prison in July 1991.

Sometimes it's not training that causes problems but bias. Science is supposed to be neutral. But most forensic chemists work for labs linked to government-funded police departments. That puts them on the same "team" as the police and prosecutors. Some experts argue that this might lead chemists to be biased toward helping secure a conviction. In some cases, labs are paid only if a suspect pleads guilty or is convicted. According to journalist Radley Balko, these labs are "literally being paid to provide the analysis to win convictions. Their findings are then presented to juries as the careful ... work of an objective scientist."

Even more disturbing to many are the cases of malpractice. Annie Dookhan was a chemist with a Massachusetts state drug lab. In 2012, she was found to have purposely falsified test results. She also wrote up reports for tests she never performed. Her goal was to impress her bosses with her efficient performance. She could "analyze" 500 samples a month, compared with her coworkers' 50 to 150 samples. During her career, Dookhan signed off on more than 60,000 samples from 34,000 criminal cases. Many people who were convicted in those cases have now been released because of Dookhan's questionable analysis of the evidence.

Arson investigation has also met with problems in recent years. Investigators once believed that arson fires created specific, puddle-shaped burn patterns on the floor. Based on such patterns, Texan Cameron Todd Willingham was executed in 2004. He had been convicted of setting fire to his home, killing his three young daughters. But authorities now believe the fire started accidentally. They say traces of accelerant that had been

OPPOSITE In 2015, shortly before the 20th anniversary of a terrorist attack that had left 13 dead and more than 6,300 ill, the Tokyo fire department conducted a simulated gas attack to measure its antiterrorism responsiveness.

identified as mineral spirits were likely from a bottle of charcoal lighter fluid on the home's porch. The bottle likely spilled when hit by the blast of the firefighters' hose.

The biggest issue, many say, is the lack of oversight of forensic operations in general. In 2014, the National Commission on Forensic Science (NCFS) was organized to recommend quality control and training requirements. But some say further reform is needed. They want lab tests to be monitored by video. Some are pushing for an independent crime lab system, separate from other police and government agencies.

Even as they work to improve their current methods, forensic chemists have to keep alert to future dangers. Some see mass poisonings as the next great chemical threat. Such poisonings could be carried out by terrorists. The poison could be spread through food, water, or the

air. The world got a taste of what such poisonings might be like in 1995 when sarin gas was released on a subway in Tokyo. In 2001, letters containing anthrax were sent to American politicians and news media, causing a scare.

Forensic scientists also have to keep up to date with the designer drugs constantly being created. These drugs often require the development of new tests. New methods are also being developed to test for common drugs such as marijuana and heroin. Some tests now detect these drugs in sweat collected on a patch worn on the skin. Saliva swabs are being developed for drug testing as well. Chemists are also working on ways to detect explosive residue, drugs, and other chemicals in fingerprints.

Forensic chemistry continues to advance with each new testing method. But its goal of analyzing substances to solve crimes remains the same. "If a person has been murdered, then we're his last resource," says FBI chemist Bob Forgione. "If we don't find out what happened, the truth is going to be buried with that person." He and other forensic chemists are dedicated to making sure that doesn't happen.

Glossary

atoms
: the smallest units of an element (a substance that cannot be broken apart into simpler substances)

barbiturates
: depressant drugs often used as sedatives or sleeping pills

bile
: a bitter, yellow-brown fluid secreted by the liver to aid in digestion

compounds
: substances made up of atoms of two or more elements that are chemically combined

contaminating
: introducing foreign material

designer drug
: a synthetic drug designed to have a slightly different molecular structure from an illegal substance

electrons
: minuscule, negatively charged particles that travel around the nucleus of an atom

entomologist
: a scientist who studies insects

exhumed
: removed from a grave

gas chromatographs
: instruments used to separate a sample into its component gases

genetic
: having to do with genes, which transfer traits from a parent to a child

improvised
explosive devices also known as IEDs, homemade bombs
made with nonmilitary materials and often
used by terrorists to injure or kill

litmus paper a special paper used to test whether a
substance is an acid or a base

mass
spectrometers devices that break chemicals apart into
charged particles and then put those
particles through a magnetic or electric
field, which causes them to spread out into
a distinctive pattern that can be used to
identify the substance

medical examiner a doctor who examines dead bodies to
determine the cause of suspicious or
unnatural deaths

molecules the smallest units of an element or
compound that can exist on their own and
still have the properties of that element or
compound

opiates natural or manmade sedative drugs
derived from opium, which is made from
the opium poppy

organic having to do with compounds consisting of
carbon

reagents chemicals that react with other substances
to detect or measure the substances

vaporizes turns into a gas

Selected Bibliography

Dale, W. Mark, and Wendy S. Becker. *The Crime Scene: How Forensic Science Works*. New York: Kaplan, 2007.

Fisher, Barry A. J. *Techniques of Crime Scene Investigation*. 7th ed. Boca Raton, Fla.: CRC Press, 2004.

Fisher, David. *Hard Evidence: How Detectives Inside the FBI's Sci-Crime Lab Have Helped Solve America's Toughest Cases*. New York: Simon & Schuster, 1995.

National Forensic Science Technology Center. *A Simplified Guide to Forensic Science*. http://www.forensicsciencesimplified.org/index.htm.

Owen, David. *Hidden Evidence: 50 True Crimes and How Forensic Science Helped Solve Them*. 2nd ed. Buffalo, N.Y.: Firefly Books, 2009.

Ramsland, Katherine. *The C.S.I. Effect*. New York: Berkley Boulevard, 2006.

Ricciuti, Edward. *Science 101: Forensics*. New York: HarperCollins, 2007.

Swanson, Charles R., Neil C. Chamelin, Leonard Territo, and Robert W. Taylor. *Criminal Investigation*. 9th ed. New York: McGraw-Hill, 2006.

Websites

CSI: The Experience Web Adventures
http://forensics.rice.edu/

Try your hand as a toxicologist or fire investigator through interactive games and training sessions.

PBS: Tales from the Poisoner's Handbook
http://www.pbs.org/wgbh/americanexperience/features/interactive/poisoners-tales/

See if you can solve these real-life poisoning cases.

Note: Every effort has been made to ensure that any websites listed above were active at the time of publication. However, because of the nature of the Internet, it is impossible to guarantee that these sites will remain active indefinitely or that their contents will not be altered.

Index